SCHOLASTIC

READ & RESPOND

Bringing the best books to life in the classroom

CW00515154

Activities based on

Why the Whales Came

By Michael Morpurgo

Terms and conditions

IMPORTANT – PERMITTED USE AND WARNINGS – READ CAREFULLY BEFORE USING

IF YOU ACCEPT THE ABOVE CONDITIONS YOU MAY PROCEED TO USE THE CD-ROM.

Recommended system requirements:
Windows: XP (Service Pack 3), Vista (Service Pack 2), Windows 7 or Windows 8 with 2.33GHz processor
Mac: OS 10.6 to 10.8 with Intel Core™ Duo processor
1GB RAM (recommended)
1024 × 768 Screen resolution
CD-ROM drive (24× speed recommended)
Adobe Reader (version 9 recommended for Mac users)
Broadband internet connections (for installation and updates)

For all technical support queries (including no CD drive), please phone Scholastic Customer Services on 0845 6039091.

Designed using Adobe Indesign
Scholastic Education, an imprint of Scholastic Ltd
Book End, Range Road, Witney, Oxfordshire, OX29 0YD
Registered office: Westfield Road, Southam, Warwickshire, CV47 0RA

Printed and bound by Ashford Colour Press
© 2017 Scholastic Ltd
1 2 3 4 5 6 7 8 9   7 8 9 0 1 2 3 4 5 6

British Library Cataloguing-in-Publication Data
A catalogue record for this book is available from the British Library.
ISBN 978-1407-16068-9

Extracts from *The National Curriculum in England, English Programme of Study* © Crown Copyright. Reproduced under the terms of the Open Government Licence (OGL). http://www.nationalarchives.gov.uk/doc/open-government-licence/version/3

Due to the nature of the web, we cannot guarantee the content or links of any site mentioned. We strongly recommend that teachers check websites before using them in the classroom.

Author Jillian Powell
Editorial team Rachel Morgan, Jenny Wilcox, Kate Pedlar and Jennie Clifford
Series designer Neil Salt
Designer Alice Duggan
Illustrator Dave Smith/Beehive Illustration
Digital development Hannah Barnett, Phil Crothers and MWA Technologies Private Ltd

Acknowledgements
The publishers gratefully acknowledge permission to reproduce the following copyright material:

Egmont UK Limited for permission to use the cover and text extracts from *Why The Whales Came* by Michael Morpurgo. Text copyright © 1985 Michael Morpurgo. Cover images 2011 © Shutterstock. Published by Egmont UK Limited and used with permission.

Every effort has been made to trace copyright holders for the works reproduced in this book, and the publishers apologise for any inadvertent omissions.

CONTENTS ▼

▼ INTRODUCTION

Read & Respond provides teaching ideas related to a specific children's book. The series focuses on best-loved books and brings you ways to use them to engage your class and enthuse them about reading.

The book is divided into different sections.

- **About the book and author:** gives you some background information about the book and the author.

- **Guided reading:** breaks the book down into sections and gives notes for using it with guided reading groups. A bookmark has been provided on page 12 containing comprehension questions. The children can be directed to refer to these as they read.

- **Shared reading:** provides extracts from the children's book with associated notes for focused work. There is also one non-fiction extract that relates to the children's book.

- **Grammar, punctuation & spelling:** provides word-level work related to the children's book so you can teach grammar, punctuation and spelling in context.

- **Plot, character & setting:** contains activity ideas focused on the plot, characters and the setting of the story.

- **Talk about it:** has speaking and listening activities related to the children's book. These activities may be based directly on the children's book or be broadly based on the themes and concepts of the story.

- **Get writing:** provides writing activities related to the children's book. These activities may be based directly on the children's book or be broadly based on the themes and concepts of the story.

- **Assessment:** contains short activities that will help you assess whether the children have understood the concepts and curriculum objectives. They are designed to be informal activities to feed into your planning.

The activities follow the same format.

- **Objective:** the objective for the lesson. It will be based upon a curriculum objective, but will often be more specific to the focus being covered.

- **What you need:** a list of resources you need to teach the lesson, including digital resources (printable pages, interactive activities and media resources, see page 5).

- **What to do:** the activity notes.

- **Differentiation:** this is provided where specific and useful differentiation advice can be given to support and/or extend the learning in the activity. Differentiation by providing additional adult support has not been included as this will be at a teacher's discretion based upon specific children's needs and ability, as well as the availability of support.

The activities are numbered for reference within each section and should move through the text sequentially – so you can use the lesson while you are reading the book. Once you have read the book, most of the activities can be used in any order you wish.

Below are brief guidance notes for using the CD-ROM. For more detailed information, please click on the '?' button in the top right-hand corner of the screen.

The program contains:
- the extract pages from the book
- all of the photocopiable pages from the book
- additional printable pages
- interactive on-screen activities
- media resources.

Getting started

Put the CD-ROM into your CD-ROM drive. If you do not have a CD-ROM drive, phone Scholastic Customer Services on 0845 6039091.

- For Windows users, the install wizard should autorun. If it fails to do so, then navigate to your CD-ROM drive and follow the installation process.
- For Mac users, copy the disk image file to your hard drive. After it has finished copying, double-click it to mount the disk image. Navigate to the mounted disk image and run the installer. After installation, the disk image can be unmounted and the DMG can be deleted from the hard drive.
- To install on a network, see the ReadMe file located on the CD-ROM (navigate to your drive).

To complete the installation of the program, you need to open the program and click 'Update' in the pop-up. Please note – this CD-ROM is web-enabled and the content will be downloaded from the internet to your hard drive to populate the CD-ROM with the relevant resources. This only needs to be done on first use; after this you will be able to use the CD-ROM without an internet connection. If at any point any content is updated, you will receive another pop-up upon start up when there is an internet connection.

Main menu

The Main menu is the first screen that appears. Here you can access: terms and conditions, registration links, how to use the CD-ROM, and credits. To access a specific book, click on the relevant button (only titles installed will be available). You can filter by the drop-down lists if you wish. You can search all resources by clicking 'Search' in the bottom left-hand corner. You can also log in and access favourites that you have bookmarked.

Resources

By clicking on a book on the Main menu, you are taken to the resources for that title. The resources are: Media, Interactives, Extracts, and Printables. Select the category and then launch a resource by clicking the 'Play' button.

Teacher settings

In the top right-hand corner of the screen is a small 'T' icon. This is the teacher settings area. It is password protected, and the password is: login. This area will allow you to choose the print quality settings for interactive activities ('Default' or 'Best') and also allow you to check for updates to the program or re-download all content to the disk via 'Refresh all content'. You can also set up user logins so that you can save and access favourites. Once a user is set up, they can enter by clicking the login link underneath the 'T' and '?' buttons.

Search

You can access an all-resources search by clicking the 'Search' button on the bottom left of the Main menu. You can search for activities by type (using the drop-down filter) or by keyword by typing into the box. You can then assign resources to your favourites area or launch them directly from the search area.

CURRICULUM LINKS

Section	Activity	Curriculum objectives
Guided reading		Spoken language: To develop understanding through speculating, hypothesising, imagining, and exploring ideas; to participate in discussions, presentations, performances, role play, improvisations and debates.
Shared reading	1	Comprehension: To discuss words and phrases that capture the reader's interest and imagination.
	2	Comprehension: To discuss words and phrases that capture the reader's interest and imagination.
	3	Comprehension: To discuss words and phrases that capture the reader's interest and imagination; to identify how language, structure and presentation contribute to meaning.
	4	Comprehension: To discuss words and phrases that capture the reader's interest and imagination; to retrieve and record information from non-fiction.
Grammar, punctuation & spelling	1	Composition: To extend the range of sentences with more than one clause by using a wider range of conjunctions, including 'when', 'if', 'because', 'although'.
	2	Composition: To use fronted adverbials.
	3	Transcription: To spell further homophones.
	4	Composition: To choose nouns or pronouns appropriately for clarity and cohesion and to avoid repetition.
	5	Composition: To use and punctuate direct speech.
	6	Transcription: To write from memory simple sentences dictated by the teacher, that include words and punctuation taught so far.
Plot, character & setting	1	Composition: To create settings, characters and plot in narratives.
	2	Comprehension: To draw inferences such as inferring characters' feelings, thoughts and motives from their actions, and justifying inferences with evidence.
	3	Comprehension: To draw inferences such as inferring characters' feelings, thoughts and motives from their actions and justifying inferences with evidence.
	4	Comprehension: To ask questions to improve their understanding of a text, to draw inferences, and justify inferences with evidence, such as inferring characters' feelings, thoughts and motives from their actions.
	5	Comprehension: To draw inferences, justifying inferences with evidence; to identify themes and conventions in a wide range of books.
	6	Spoken language: To use spoken language to develop understanding through speculating, hypothesising, imagining and exploring ideas. Comprehension: To identify themes and conventions in a wide range of books.
	7	Comprehension: To identify main ideas drawn from more than one paragraph and summarising these.
	8	Comprehension: To identify themes and conventions in a wide range of books.

Section	Activity	Curriculum objectives
Talk about it	1	Spoken language: To articulate and justify answers, arguments and opinions; to use spoken language to develop understanding through speculating, hypothesising, imagining and exploring ideas.
	2	Spoken language: To use spoken language to develop understanding through speculating, hypothesising, imagining and exploring ideas. Comprehension: To draw inferences such as inferring characters' feelings, thoughts and motives from their actions, and justifying inferences with evidence.
	3	Spoken language: To participate in discussions, presentations, performances, role play, improvisations and debates.
	4	Spoken language: To use spoken language to develop understanding through exploring ideas; to participate in discussions.
	5	Spoken language: To use spoken language to develop understanding through speculating, hypothesising, imagining and exploring ideas.
	6	Spoken language: To participate in discussions and role play; to consider and evaluate different viewpoints.
Get writing	1	Composition: To discuss writing similar to that which they are planning to write in order to understand and learn from its structure, vocabulary and grammar; to use simple organisational devices in non-narrative material.
	2	Comprehension: To learn the conventions of different types of writing (for example, a diary written in the first person).
	3	Composition: To discuss writing similar to that which they are planning to write in order to understand and learn from its structure, vocabulary and grammar; to create settings, character and plot in narratives.
	4	Comprehension: To prepare poems and playscripts to read aloud and to perform, showing understanding through intonation, tone, volume and action.
	5	Comprehension: To retrieve and record information from non-fiction. Composition: To organise paragraphs around a theme.
	6	Composition: To discuss and record ideas; to use simple organisational devices in non-narrative material (for example, headings and subheadings).
Assessment	1	Comprehension: To draw inferences such as inferring characters' thoughts feelings and motives from their actions, and justifying these with evidence. Spoken language: To participate in discussions; to use spoken language to develop understanding through imagining and exploring ideas.
	2	Spoken language: To use spoken language to develop understanding through speculating, hypothesising, imagining and exploring ideas.
	3	Comprehension: To prepare poems and playscripts to read aloud and to perform, showing understanding through intonation, tone, volume and action.
	4	Comprehension: To identify themes and conventions in a wide range of books.
	5	Composition: To use and punctuate direct speech.
	6	Spoken language: To articulate and justify answers, arguments and opinions; to participate in discussions and presentations.

WHY THE WHALES CAME

About the book

Why the Whales Came (1985) is set on the island of Bryher, in the Isles of Scilly, where author Michael Morpurgo has spent his summer holidays for more than 20 years. This atmospheric island setting was also used for his novels *Arthur: High King of Britain* (1994), *The Wreck of the Zanzibar* (1995) and *The Sleeping Sword* (2002).

The setting in *Why the Whales Came* contributes to many of the author's key themes: the close, yet sometimes claustrophobic, nature of a tight-knit island community; the way the islanders' lives are ruled by the sea and the weather; and the interdependent relationship between them and the natural world. As in *The Wreck of the Zanzibar,* the islanders' treatment of the wildlife with which they share their environment seems to determine their destiny – good or bad.

Why the Whales Came is the story of two young friends, Gracie and Daniel, who are warned to stay away from the mysterious and feared 'Birdman' who lives alone on the other side of Bryher. Just when it looks as if the islanders are about to take violent action against the Birdman (whom they suspect of being a war spy), the stranding of a whale on the beach results in a crisis, then reconciliation and, finally, the lifting of the island curse. As in another of Michael Morpurgo's books, *Kensuke's Kingdom* (1999), the story features an unlikely friendship which, in this case, transcends barriers of age, deafness, rumour and prejudice.

Michael Morpurgo's stories are often based on real-life events. In *Why the Whales Came*, he embellishes the history of the island of Samson with a mysterious curse; in real life, the island became uninhabited when the last residents were evicted by the Lord Proprietor of the Isles of Scilly in 1855. Like *War Horse* and *Private Peaceful* (also by Michael Morpurgo), the story is set against the background of World War I (1914–1918) and shows how the war affected and changed lives, even on remote islands like the Isles of Scilly.

About the author

Michael Morpurgo was born in St Albans in 1943. At school, he really enjoyed rugby and singing.

He began writing for children when he was a teacher, encouraged by the children's responses to stories he read to them. His first book was published in 1975. He has since had more than 100 books and several screenplays published, and his works have been translated into 26 different languages. He writes in an exercise book, propped up on pillows on his bed, and says, 'I write for the child in me, I write for the adolescent in me, I write for the adult in me, I write for the old [person] in me'.

Michael Morpurgo has won many awards for his children's books (including the Smarties Book Prize, the Whitbread Children's Book Award, and the British Book Awards Children's Book of the Year), and has had books adapted for stage and television.

He lives near Iddesleigh in Devon, where he set up the charity *Farms for City Children* with his wife, Clare. He began this project in 1976, to give city children experience of life on a farm; there are now three farms that children can visit.

Michael Morpurgo was awarded the MBE in 1999 and the OBE in 2006; he was Children's Laureate from 2003 to 2005.

Key facts

Why the Whales Came
Author: Michael Morpurgo
First published: 1985 by William Heinemann
Did you know?: In the 1989 film adaptation of *When the Whales Came,* Gracie was played by island girl Helen Pearce. The novel was also adapted into a stage play by Theatre Alibi and was staged in 2001 and 2003.

First reading

Look together at the cover of *Why the Whales Came*, and then read the back-cover blurb. Ask: *What sort of story do you think this will be – adventure, thriller, mystery? Who do you think the mysterious figure shown on the cover might be? What is the main 'hook' in the blurb that makes the reader want to read the story?* Look at the map of the islands and read the 'preface' note written by the character Gracie. Ask the children what these tell them before they start to read the story. (It is set on the Isles of Scilly, and is about a young girl called Gracie.) Ask the children to work out Gracie's age as she writes (81 – the book was first published in 1985) and if they know the significance of the date 1914 (it was the year World War I, known as the Great War, started).

Chapter 1

Read the first chapter together as far as the paragraph ending 'indeed he scarcely even looked at anyone'. Pause to ask the children why the west coast of the island is 'forbidden territory' and why they think the mysterious man is known as 'the Birdman'. (He is always followed by a flock of seagulls.) Read almost to the end of the chapter, as far as the line 'I knew well enough who that someone must be'. Ask the children what Gracie and Daniel assume. (That the Birdman has taken their boats.) Read on to the end of the chapter. Ask: *What do you think the letters in the sand might be?* (They are Birdman's initials.)

Chapter 2

Read on through Chapter 2. Ask: *Why does everyone fear Samson?* (It is said to be cursed.) *What do you think 'unredeemed guilt' might mean?* (Something bad happened there which has not been put right, and has invoked the punishment of a curse.) Ask: *How do the islanders see the Birdman? What happens that makes Gracie and Daniel see him in another light?* (He leaves them a gift on the beach.) Refer to question 1 on the Guided Reading bookmark.

Chapter 3

Read on, pausing at the first mention of war to ask the children if they know which war this refers to (World War I, or the Great War, 1914–1918, which was fought between Britain and her allies against Germany and her allies). Continue to the end of the chapter, and ask the children how Gracie and Daniel have learned to communicate with the Birdman. (They leave messages in the sand.)

Chapters 4 and 5

Continue reading through Chapters 4 and 5. Ask: *What do the children discover about the Birdman when they meet him?* (He is deaf.) *What important news does he give them?* (Timber has been washed up onto the beach.) Ask question 2 on the Guided Reading bookmark. Can they explain why Gracie is so worried when her father finds the cormorant and why Daniel pretends he made it? (They know their parents will be furious if they find out they have been seeing the Birdman.) Discuss question 12 on the bookmark.

Chapters 6 and 7

Read these next two chapters, pausing at the end of Chapter 6. Discuss question 3 on the Guided Reading bookmark. Ask the children to recap all the ways the war has changed the islanders' lives. At the end of Chapter 7, consider the cliffhanger that makes the reader want to read on. Refer to question 8 on the bookmark.

Chapters 8 and 9

Read Chapter 8, pausing to ask questions 13 and 14 on the Guided Reading bookmark. Continue through Chapter 9 and then recap on the two unhappy events that unfold. (Big Tim and his gang bully Daniel and Gracie, and suspect the Birdman of spying; Gracie's father goes missing.) Ask question 4 on the bookmark. Ask: *What do you understand by the last line of the chapter?* (Gracie thinks that by going to Samson they have brought the curse upon themselves, which is why her father has gone missing.)

Chapters 10 and 11

Continue through Chapter 10, pausing to ask the first part of question 15 on the Guided Reading bookmark. Read on to the end of Chapter 11. Ask the children to summarise what we learn about the reason for the curse on Samson. Ask: *What does the Birdman fear now?* (He fears that Bryher will suffer the same curse if Big Tim and his gang kill the stranded whale.) Tell the children that, in real life, Samson has been uninhabited since the last residents were evicted in 1855 by Augustus Smith, the Lord Proprietor of the Isles of Scilly, who tried creating a deer park there – although the deer later escaped.

Chapter 12

Finish reading the story; then ask the children if they can interpret what has happened. (The curse has been redeemed by saving the whales.) Challenge children to respond to questions 6 and 16 on the Guided Reading bookmark.

Second reading

Before reading the book again, consider what sort of story the children think this is. Adventure? Mystery? Encourage them to give reasons for their answers. Consider the structure of the book and focus on question 7 on the Guided Reading bookmark. Re-read the first paragraph together and discuss why it is an effective opening. (It creates a mood of fear and mystery, and offers us a 'hook' because we know the children ignore the warning.) Consider question 11 on the bookmark. Pause at the end of the first chapter and ask the children if they can recall some of the images the author creates by his descriptive writing – the scenery of the island, the busy activity on the beach, the haunting image of the Birdman in his cart with the seagulls wheeling around in the sky above his head. Raise question 10 on the bookmark, encouraging the children to recall or find other episodes where imagery aids description in the novel (for example, the fog descending).

Island life

Re-read Chapters 2, 3 and 4. Ask the children to summarise some of the views different characters express about the Birdman, and what we have learned about him by the end of the section. Next, re-read Chapter 5. Ask: *What does the timber episode tells us about the islanders?* (They are not well off and so salvage what they can to help them survive, even if they have to lie to the authorities.) Briefly discuss some of the features about island life that are emerging. (It's a close community that sticks together, but one that can foster rumour, superstitions and even false prejudices.)

The Great War

Begin re-reading Chapter 6, pausing at the first paragraph to ask what the children understand by 'the Front in France' (the fighting lines in northern France where the opposing armies faced each other). Ask: *What do you know about the Great War? Do you know of any relatives who fought in the war? Have you seen any films or pictures of the trenches?* Read on through Chapter 7, as far as 'and I knew Daniel would need little persuasion' and then pause to review how the war has changed the lives of the people who live on the islands. (There are blackouts at night, the fear of invasion/submarines, husbands and fathers joining up, children no longer having time for carefree play, and so on.)

Samson

Read on into Chapter 8, pausing at the mention of 'smugglers and wreckers' to check if the children understand what these were (people who illegally imported goods to avoid paying duty, or deliberately wrecked ships so they could salvage the cargo). Refer to question 9 on the Guided Reading bookmark. Ask the children why Gracie is so scared when they realise they are on Samson. Continue to the end of the chapter and discuss Gracie's and Daniel's reactions to being stranded: Daniel is down to earth and matter of fact, while Gracie is full of the superstition and fears that her father and others have instilled in her. Return to question 11 on the bookmark.

Conflict

Re-read Chapter 9 as far as the end of Gracie's dream, pausing for the children to identify the memories that have become woven together or muddled up in her dream (the mysterious horn, her father at sea, the fog). Then read on to the end of the bullying incident with Big Tim. Ask the children to explain what the Birdman is being accused of (collaborating with the Germans). Explain that, during both World Wars, collaboration with the enemy was seen as a serious offence. Ask: *Why do you think the Birdman is being picked on?* (He is an outsider, lives alone and is misunderstood.) *What is he accused of doing and what is he doing in reality?* (The islanders think he is signalling to German submarines; in reality, he is lighting a beacon to warn ships in bad weather.) Continue reading to the end of Chapter 10. Then discuss the conflict that takes place: what does each side want to do, and why? (Big Tim and his gang want to drive the Birdman off the island for being a spy, and kill the whales for their meat and ivory; the Birdman wants to rescue the whales and so redeem the curse on Samson.)

Resolution

Read to the end of the novel. Discuss with the children how and why the mood of the islanders is turned around. (Gracie's mother speaks out in defence of the Birdman, allowing Daniel to tell the Birdman's story.) Return to question 15 on the Guided Reading bookmark. Ask: *How is the curse on Samson lifted?* (The islanders rescue the narwhals, thus redeeming them from the curse that came about from the massacre of whales when the Birdman was a boy.) Ask: *What comes good as a result?* (Gracie's father returns home, the well on Samson is no longer dry and the islanders no longer fear the curse.) Discuss whether the children think it is a satisfactory ending, and why. Ask question 5 on the bookmark. Finally, allude to the final paragraph of the novel, which addresses the reader, and discuss which elements of the story the children think are fictional (such as characters and plot) and which are real (such as the setting, backdrop of World War I and the fact that the last families left Samson in the 1850s, leaving the island uninhabited).

SCHOLASTIC

READ&RESPOND

Bringing the best books to life in the classroom

Why the Whales Came
by Michael Morpurgo

SCHOLASTIC

READ&RESPOND

Bringing the best books to life in the classroom

Why the Whales Came
by Michael Morpurgo

Focus on...
Meaning

1. What does finding the carved cormorant tell the children about the Birdman?

2. Why is Gracie mortified when her father discovers the cormorant?

3. What are the two chief reasons why Mr Jenkins takes the King's Shilling?

4. Why does Big Tim suspect the Birdman is a spy for the Germans? What is the Birdman really trying to do?

5. How does the story tell us about the author's attitude towards the natural world? Can you suggest any parallels in other novels by the author?

Focus on...
Organisation

6. How much time do you think passes during the main narrative? Find clues.

7. Look at the chapter headings. Explain how each heading relates to the chapter content.

8. How does the author create suspense at the end of Chapters 3, 7 and 10?

Focus on...
Language and features

9. Note any examples of nautical (sailing) or maritime (sea) terms.

10. How does the author use imagery to enhance description of the setting? Find examples.

Focus on...
Purpose, viewpoints and effects

11. Who is the story's narrator? What difference might it make if Daniel were narrating?

12. What makes the Birdman seem strange or scary? What makes him seem friendly and kind?

13. What clues to Samson's history do the children discover on the island?

14. What is the significance of the horn that the children discover in a ruined cottage on Samson?

15. Why does the Birdman take gifts to Mrs Jenkins? How is his kindness repaid in the end?

16. Does the story have a fairytale 'happy ending'? Cite evidence.

Extract 1

- This extract is from Chapter 5 and describes the exciting events on the island after the children return with the news the Birdman has shared with them: that a boatload of timber has been washed ashore at Popplestones. *Ask: Why are the islanders so excited?* (They can recover the cargo of timber and use it – perhaps for houses and boat building.) *Can you explain why the Preventative would stop the islanders taking the timber?* (It is officially the property of the Crown and it would be a crime to take it or hide it away.)

- Invite the children to pick out all the things mentioned here that the sea provides, exploring any unfamiliar words ('seaweed', 'driftwood', 'trove').

- Underline the phrase 'high-water mark' and ask the children to explain its meaning. Briefly discuss the idea of tides and the way they are controlled by the moon's cycles. Circle the words 'harvest', 'fished' and 'windfall'. *Ask: What do these words usually describe? How are they used metaphorically here?* (The islanders pull cargo out of the sea just as they catch fish; the timber is like a 'crop' of wood from the sea; it is blown ashore by the wind, just as the wind blows fruit from trees.)

- Focus on the verbs, highlighting all the passive phrases: 'was littered', 'had been smashed', 'lay splintered', 'was scattered', 'was smothered'. *Ask: Can you suggest why passive verbs are used here?* (They emphasise the timber being at the mercy of the elements.)

- Ask the children to identify a metaphor and explain what it describes. (The description 'a heaving, groaning blanket of boards' suggests the boards are completely covering the sea like a blanket but, unlike a normal blanket, they are also creaking and groaning as they knock together.)

Extract 2

- Extract 2 is from Chapter 7 and leads into the most exciting and adventurous episode in the story, where the children become lost in their small boat in the fog. Read the extract together and ask the children to summarise Gracie and Daniel's predicament. (Their boat is suddenly becalmed in fog.) *Ask: Which sentence emphasises the sudden impact of the fog?* ('Scilly rock had vanished as had the sky and the sea as well.')

- Circle any words that may be unfamiliar, including nautical terms such as 'becalmed' and 'astern', and invite the children to offer explanations as to their meaning. *Ask: Which verbs and adjectives create the feeling of being becalmed?* ('lolled', 'lapped', 'listless')

- Revise alliteration, circling the alliterative phrases: 'lapped by a listless sea', 'a silent sea', 'the sea slapped so softly' and 'the surge of the sea seething'. Remind the children that these phrases are onomatopoeic, imitating the soft sounds of the sea. *Ask: Why should sound be the most important sense in this description?* (The children can't see anything because of the fog.) How might sound help them get home? (If they can hear the sea around Scilly Rock they can find their way back.)

- Ask the children to find an example of a metaphor that the writer uses? ('grey wall of fog') Circle the phrase 'as if the fog were a living creature' and invite the children to pick out the words and phrases that personify the fog as well as the sea (for example, 'lolled', 'listless'). Invite them to invent more phrases or sentences that personify the fog or the sea.

Extract 3

- This extract is from Chapter 11 and relates the final effort, led by the Birdman, to prevent the pod of whales beaching themselves. Read the extract together and ask the children what the Birdman is desperate to do and why. (He wants to stop the whales from becoming beached, because he thinks it is the only way to lift the curse of Samson and prevent Bryher being cursed too.)

- Circle any words that may be unfamiliar to the children ('ashen', 'flailing', 'frenzy'). Can they suggest the meaning, identify the part of speech (noun, adjective, verb and so on) and offer replacements? Underline the phrase 'in a pack' and ask the children if they know the correct collective term for whales (a pod).

- Examine the language features that the author uses to convey a sense of urgency. Highlight the repetition of words and phrases and ask: *Why do you think the Birdman repeats the word 'fire' four times?* (He is registering what is driving the whales away, thinking aloud, and wants to convey this as fast and as powerfully as he can.) Focus on the sentence that begins with multiple nouns ('Flaming torches, oil lamps…') considering how the word order contributes to a sense of chaos and panic.

- Ask: *Why must the children now stay on the beach?* (It is now dark and the sea is rough.) How long do the children estimate this episode has lasted? Encourage them to cite evidence. (It is light when it begins and then night falls; the Birdman is exhausted from strenuous efforts, and so on.)

- Highlight poetic description that makes the scene more vivid, pointing out features such as assonance ('whales' flailing tails') and imagery ('the sea whipped up into a frenzy').

Extract 4

- This non-fiction extract is written in the style of a brochure aimed at visitors to the Isles of Scilly, explaining how they can reach Samson and other islands by sea kayak.

- Read the extract together and ask the children who they think the text is aimed at. (active or sporty visitors to the Isles of Scilly)

- Ask them to explain why the sea kayak would be the best way of exploring the islands. (It is small and easily manoeuvred and so can access shallow waters where bigger boats can't go.)

- Circle any unfamiliar vocabulary ('azure', 'isthmus', 'malnutrition', 'eviction', 'cairns') and ask the children if they can explain them and suggest alternative words or phrases to replace them.

- Challenge the children to find examples of similes ('shimmers like azure silk', 'gaping like missing teeth') and metaphor/imagery ('forests of seaweed,' 'cottages that huddle', 'graves that stud the sacred hills', squawks that 'burst the air', graves 'cloaked with massive capstones'). Discuss how these help us to visualise the scene.

- Can the children find an idiom? ('off the beaten track') Ask them to explain its meaning and suggest another way of saying it (to more remote, or less visited, places).

- Focus on all the facts about the landscape or scenery. Challenge the children to cite evidence from the novel that echoes these facts, such as: the ruined cottages the children find; the names Woodcock and Webber; the bracken, rabbits, terns and gulls; the broken clay pipe and the mound of limpet shells. Ask: *What other features of the island do we learn about from this text?* (We are told about prehistoric cairns and burial chambers, wild flowers, cowrie shells and the deer park.)

Extract 1

Chapter 5

I could see the Birdman's little boat hauled up on the dry sand, and from one end of the beach to the other the sand was littered with timber. Some of it had been smashed against the rocks and lay splintered in the water, but most of it was scattered across the beach in untidy piles and was still quite undamaged. In the farthest corner of the bay by the rocks the sea itself was smothered under a heaving, groaning blanket of boards.

Any thoughts of the war were forgotten now in this new heady excitement. No one could remember a harvest such as this, and for us on the island that is exactly what it was. Life there was never easy. We lived only on what we grew, on what we fished out of the sea, on what we made and sometimes by what we found on the beaches. Whatever was washed up by the sea on Bryher was as much ours as the fish we caught or the crops we grew. It was the way we lived, the only way we could live. Just as the seaweed and driftwood belonged to whichever of us were fortunate enough to find it and carry it above the high-water mark, so it was part of the same ancient tradition that anything, any wrecks, any cargo, any trove washed up on the shore belonged to us by right. But every child knew well that the Customs Officers over on St Mary's – the 'Preventative' as we called them – had different ideas and they would do all they could to stop us from keeping such a windfall; and there was nothing that united the islanders so much as the prospect of a visit from the Preventative. Everyone knew that morning on Popplestones that the Preventative would be coming sooner rather than later – they always did.

Extract 2

Chapter 7

We were fishing with our backs to Scilly Rock and the open sea. The boat lolled beneath us, lapped by a listless sea. I had just hooked my biggest pilchard when I noticed a wisp of mist above our heads. I looked around over my shoulder. Scilly Rock had vanished as had the sky and sea as well. A grey wall of fog was rolling in towards us over the sea. There was nothing we could do, for it was already too late to do anything. It was over us and all around us before Daniel could even haul up his line. Gweal and Bryher beyond it were not there any more and we were left alone and lost on a silent sea. What little breeze there was had gone and we found ourselves quite becalmed. I remember we spoke in a whisper, as if the fog were a living creature that might be listening to us. I was not too worried though, not at first, for the sea slapped so softly against the sides of the boat and seemed to hold no threat for us. Besides, I had Daniel with me. Both of us had been out in fog before, and both of us thought we knew the waters around Bryher quite well enough to get home.

'As long as we keep Scilly Rock astern of us we can pull home easily enough,' Daniel said softly.

'But how are we going to do that if we can't see it?' I whispered, taking the oar he was handing me. 'I can't see it any more.'

'We can hear it though, can't we?' he said. 'Listen.' And certainly I could hear the surge of the sea seething around Scilly Rock as it always did even on the calmest of days. 'Hear it?' he said. 'Just keep that sound astern of us and we will be able to feel our way home.'

Extract 3

Chapter 11

The Birdman, Daniel and I were sitting drinking our soup by the fire when the Birdman had the idea. His face was ashen with cold and exhaustion, but suddenly there was an urgency in his voice. 'Look where they are,' he said, getting to his feet and pointing out into the bay. 'Look at them.' The whales were lying together in a pack in the dark waters on the far side of Popplestones. 'It's the fire,' he said. 'It's the fire. They're as far from the fire as they can be. They don't like fire.'

Flaming torches, oil lamps, piles of burning brushwood and driftwood, we used anything, anything that would burn. We lit fires all along the rocks around the bay; and then the Birdman, with a long line of islanders on either side of him waving their torches above their heads, waded out into the sea towards the whales. We children were told to stay on the beach. It was too dangerous now, out in the dark water with the whales' flailing tails and the sea whipped up into a frenzy by a fresh offshore wind. So we stayed and watched the line of torches as they moved out into the bay.

Extract 4

Visit Samson by Sea Kayak!

There's no better way to explore the Isles of Scilly than by boat, and the shallow waters between the islands make a sea kayak the ideal way to get off the beaten track.

On a fine day, when the sea shimmers like azure silk, you can visit Samson, the largest uninhabited island of the Isles of Scilly. Paddle along the south coast of Tresco, then head south-west, through the shallow waters where even the flat-bottomed pleasure boats can't venture at low tide. During very low tides you can walk between Samson and Tresco.

once treasured as currency by ancient peoples, on the soft sandy beach.

Follow black peaty tracks through head-high bracken to find the romantic ruins of the 19 stone cottages that huddle on the narrow isthmus between the north and south hills. They stand with their roofs open to the skies, windows and doors gaping like missing teeth. You might find fragments of a clay pipe, or a mound of limpet shells left outside. Malnutrition forced the eviction of the last-remaining inhabitants, the Woodcock and Webber families, in 1855. The Lord Proprietor, Augustus Smith, then created a deer park here and the remains of the park wall can still be seen, along with the prehistoric cairns and chamber graves that stud the sacred hills. Cloaked with massive capstones, they face east to catch the rising sun's rays.

When the sea is calm, on the approach to Tresco you can see down to depths of five metres or more as you glide over forests of seaweed known as mermaid's hair. Beach the kayak on Samson (pull it well up the beach if the tide is coming in) and explore the island. Look out for cowrie shells,

You will see an abundance of wild flowers, such as heathers, sea campion and thrift. Your only company may be the scampering rabbits and rowdy gulls and terns that burst the air with their noisy squawks as they banter and jostle for nesting sites. Enjoy the solitude before you push off and head towards Tresco, past Puffin Island.

GRAMMAR, PUNCTUATION & SPELLING

1. Clever clauses

Objective

To extend the range of sentences with more than one clause using conjunctions.

What you need

Copies of *Why the Whales Came*.

What to do

- Write on the board some short, factual sentences about the Birdman, such as:
  - The Birdman wore a black cape.
  - The Birdman rode out in a donkey cart.
  - The Birdman collected driftwood.
  - The Birdman loved to carve birds.

- Tell the children that they are going to try extending the sentences using conjunctions. Brainstorm some possible conjunctions or connecting words, such as: after, because, although, when, while, if, where.

- Model some examples on the board, underlining or circling the conjunctions, such as: 'The Birdman wore a black cape when he rode out in his donkey cart.' 'The Birdman collected driftwood because he loved to carve birds.'

- Together brainstorm some more short, factual sentences about the Birdman and write them on the board. Explain that the children's task is to extend the sentences you have written on the board, using conjunctions.

- Arrange the class into pairs. Allow the children time to write four or five sentences. Then write the best sentences on the board, underlining or circling the conjunctions. For example: 'The Birdman had to lip read <u>when</u> the children spoke to him <u>because</u> he was deaf.'

Differentiation

Support: Provide a list of conjunctions for children to use.
Extension: Challenge pairs to write more sentences, each drafting a short sentence for their writing partner to extend using conjunctions.

2. How, when and where

Objective

To use fronted adverbials.

What you need

Interactive activity 'Which fits?', photocopiable page 22 'Which way?'

What to do

- Write on the board: Prince ran towards them. Invite the children to suggest some words or phrases to extend the sentence. Prompt them to think about when, where or how the dog ran. For example:
  - After a short while, *Prince ran towards them.* (when)
  - From across the beach, *Prince ran towards them.* (where)
  - With a wagging tail, *Prince ran towards them.* (how)

- Explain that adverbs, or phrases that act as adverbs (adverbials), can 'qualify' (tell us more about) an action. They can even change the sense completely. Demonstrate this by writing on the board:
  - With a scowl/smiling/shyly, the Birdman approached them.

- Point out that the adverbial is separated from the main clause that follows using a comma.

- As a shared activity, complete the interactive activity 'Which fits?'.

- Ask the children to complete photocopiable page 22 'Which way', in pairs. Remind them to use commas as necessary.

- When they have completed the photocopiable page, bring the class back together to share their work.

Differentiation

Support: Provide a list of adverbs or adverbial phrases to help pairs fill in the photocopiable page.
Extension: Invite children to work in pairs to draft more sentences about characters from the novel, using adverbials of time, place and manner.

3. Sounds alike

Objective
To find and spell homophones.

What you need
Photocopiable page 23 'Homophone hunt'.

What to do
- Write on the board two sentences.
  - Gracie and Daniel had to wait until the fog lifted.
  - The _____ of the whale made it hard to move.

- Revise homophones by circling or underlining the word 'wait' and then asking the children to suggest its homophone to fill the gap in the second sentence (weight).

- Brainstorm some more homophones together (or write words on the board and ask the children to find the homophone for each one) to familiarise the concept of homophones, for example, sought/sort, whole/hole, write/right, passed/past, and so on.

- Hand out photocopiable page 23 'Homophone hunt' and tell the children to work in pairs to complete it.

- Invite some children to read their sentences aloud, and challenge the class to spell each word and its homophone.

Differentiation
Support: Work together to fill in one gap for each sentence on the photocopiable sheet; provide the correct words for the children to choose from.

Extension: Working in pairs, challenge the children to draft single sentences about topics/characters from the novel that include pairs of homophones, such as 'They could hear the wails of the whales.'

4. Perfect pronouns

Objective
To choose pronouns for clarity and cohesion and to avoid repetition.

What you need
Flashcards of the names of key characters (Gracie, Daniel, the Birdman, Big Tim, Mr Wellbeloved, Mrs Jenkins, Mr Jenkins).

What to do
- Tell the children that they are going to think up short sentences about characters from the book. Hold up the flashcard 'Big Tim' and model a few examples on the board, such as:
  - Big Tim is Daniel's elder brother.
  - Big Tim is a bully.

- Arrange the children in small groups and allow them time to compose sentences about Big Tim.

- Bring the class back together and write some of the best sentences on the board. Then together arrange them in a sensible order. For example: Big Tim is Daniel's elder brother. Big Tim is a bully. Big Tim thinks the Birdman is a spy so Big Tim and Big Tim's gang ransack the Birdman's cottage.

- Underline the repeated noun/subject (Big Tim) and ask the children how they could avoid repetition (by replacing the noun with a pronoun/possessive pronoun 'he/his'). Revise the sentences using pronouns: Big Tim is Daniel's elder brother. He is a bully. He thinks the Birdman is a spy so he and his gang ransack the Birdman's cottage.

- Repeat the exercise using the other name flashcards.

Differentiation
Support: Model one or two sentences for each flashcard before the children begin working in their groups.

Extension: Groups can compose sentences starting with pronouns about other subjects from the book. They can then challenge other groups to identify them. For example: She persuades the islanders to help the whale. (Mrs Jenkins)

5. Just imagine!

Objective

To use and punctuate direct speech.

What you need

Copies of *Why the Whales Came*.

What to do

- Read the episode when Gracie's father discovers the Birdman's gift of the cormorant in the roof and goes to tackle Daniel about it (Chapter 5).

- Tell the children they are going to improvise and then draft a paragraph of direct speech or dialogue between Daniel and Mr Jenkins. They should begin by improvising the scene in pairs, with one playing the part of Daniel and the other Mr Jenkins.

- Allow them time to improvise their scenes. Then bring the class back together and extract key points from the dialogue, writing them on the board. Discuss the emotions felt: Mr Jenkins is angry and believes the children have been deceitful; Daniel knows he must think quickly to persuade Gracie's father that *he* made the cormorant. Encourage the children to think of ways to convey these emotions in written dialogue. For example:
  - 'What is the meaning of this?' Gracie's father thundered.
  - 'Oh… you found our cormorant!' Daniel said innocently.

- Discuss the use of punctuation in your example. Ask the children to write a paragraph of dialogue, using correct punctuation.

- Bring the class back together and ask volunteers to dictate their paragraph of dialogue. Write it on the board, inviting others to confirm or correct punctuation as you write. Improve the dialogue as a class activity by adding in words or punctuation.

Differentiation

Support: Model a few sentences of dialogue on the board before pairs begin their own work.
Extension: Challenge pairs to draft another dialogue, such as Mrs Jenkins telling Aunty Mildred that the children are missing.

6. Scilly spellings

Objective

To write from memory simple sentences including words and punctuation taught.

What you need

Interactive activity 'Scilly words', photocopiable page 24 'Scilly spellings', copies of *Why the Whales Came*.

What to do

- Display the interactive activity 'Scilly words' and explain that all the words are taken from the novel. Challenge the children to interpret the clues to complete the anagrams. As volunteers suggest words, invite correction or confirmation of spellings.

- Arrange the children into small groups and hand each a copy of the photocopiable page 24 'Scilly Spellings'. Tell them to read the sentences carefully because they are going to attempt writing them from dictation.

- Allow the children time to read through the sentences several times, telling them to circle or underline tricky words or spellings and note punctuation. Encourage them to think up ways to help them memorise spellings. For example, they could prompt the correct spelling of 'wrasse' by sounding the 'w'. Take back the pages before beginning dictation.

- Dictate the sentences, allowing the children time to write. When they have finished, they should check through their work against copies of the photocopiable page.

- Bring the class back together to review their work, asking for feedback on which words were most tricky to spell and which methods helped them most to memorise the words.

Differentiation

Support: Include punctuation as you dictate, to help children write their sentences.
Extension: Children can compile their own word list of the trickiest words from the novel, challenging a writing partner to spell them.

Which way?

- Write a fronted adverbial in each space provided to complete the sentences.
- Remember to use a comma.

> **For example**: <u>With a rising sense of panic</u>, Gracie and Daniel realised they were lost in the fog.

1. _____ Gracie and Daniel entered the cottage.

2. _____ Big Tim loomed over them.

3. _____ Prince ran up to them.

4. _____ Gracie and Daniel searched for a well.

5. _____ they all pushed and heaved the whale.

6. _____ they carried their torches out into the sea.

Homophone hunt

● For each pair of sentences choose a word and its homophone to fill the gaps.

Word bank

here	see	wood	missed
	hear	or	sea
oar	mist	whales	would
	sea	wood	wails

1. Gracie and Daniel were lost in the fog on the _____.

   The children could not _____ Scilly Rock or the sky or the _____.

2. The air was filled with the _____ of the seagulls.

   The Birdman realised that the _____ were moving away from the fire.

3. The Birdman was first to spot the _____ washed up at Popplestones.

   The Birdman knew the Preventative _____ seize the _____.

4. The _____ that began to form soon turned to fog.

   The children knew that as night fell they would soon be _____.

5. The Birdman was deaf so he could not _____ what they said to him.

   'The Birdman has been _____,' Daniel said.

6. When the children found the _____, they feared for the Birdman's safety.

   At first, they thought the whale horn was a lance _____ a spear.

Scilly spellings

● Check you have spelled all the words accurately and used correct punctuation.

1. Some days, to our intense disappointment, there would be nothing there but seaweed and flotsam.

2. Above him flew his usual escort of shrieking, wheeling gulls.

3. 'Hungry, were you?' came the voice from inside the sou'wester.

4. Mother and I were fishing for wrasse when we saw him bringing his boat in towards the quay.

5. Terns ruled on this island, and the night knew it of old and left us swiftly.

6. Friend and another donkey were hitched up already to the sail.

PLOT, CHARACTER & SETTING

1. Location, location

Objective
To create settings.

What you need
Printable page 'Map of Bryher, Tresco and Samson', media resource 'Images of the Isles of Scilly', copies of *Why the Whales Came*.

Cross-curricular link
Geography

What to do
- Ask the children if they can recall any island or place names from the story. Can they remember any important events in the plot that occur in the places they are able to recall?

- Arrange the children into pairs and provide them with a copy of the map on the printable page 'Map of Bryher, Tresco and Samson'. Explain to the children that they are going to link the events in the plot to the place where it occurred, for example, the whale is stranded at Popplestone Bay. Encourage the children to cite evidence from the text.

- Next, display the photographs from the media resource 'Images of the Isles of Scilly'. Invite the children to identify and describe key features: ruined cottages; house; quay; black cliffs. Encourage the children to recall how these feature in the novel, for example, the ruined cottages on Samson; Bryher church, where the service for the Birdman and Mr Jenkins is held. They should work in their pairs to annotate key locations on the map with details of local features, using the novel and photographs to help them.

Differentiation
Support: Pairs can write simple labels such as 'cliffs', 'ruined cottages'.
Extension: Encourage pairs to use the internet or books to help them provide more detail about features such as Bryher church or the local plants and wildlife.

2. Under the weather

Objective
To draw inferences and justify them with evidence.

What you need
Copies of *Why the Whales Came*, photocopiable page 29 'Turning points', scissors, paper, glue.

Cross-curricular link
Geography

What to do
- Read Chapter 7, from 'The next evening…' to the end. Ask: *What happens to make Gracie and Daniel land on forbidden Samson?* (They get stranded in their boat in thick fog.)

- Consider which weather conditions would most affect the islanders' lives (visibility, fog, storms, strong winds). Ask: *What aspects of daily life would be affected? How?* (Consider farming, fishing, going to school, and so on.)

- Ask the children to recall events in the story caused by bad weather. (Gracie and Daniel lose their boat, *Cormorant*, in windy weather at Popplestone Bay, which leads them to venture to Rushy Bay, where they meet the Birdman; they get lost in dense fog when they are out fishing). Ask: *Can you suggest any benefits that bad weather brings in the story?* (A storm blows in the timber.)

- Hand out copies of photocopiable page 29 'Turning points'. Ask the children to work in pairs to describe how each event listed moves the plot forward. When they have finished, they should cut out and glue the events in the order in which they appear in the story.

Differentiation
Support: Model one or two explanations for the photocopiable page before pairs begin work.
Extension: Encourage pairs to identify and add to the photocopiable page more turning points that drive events in the plot.

3. Truth or rumour?

To draw inferences about a character's thoughts and feelings.

Photocopiable page 30 'Truth or rumour?', copies of *Why the Whales Came*.

PSHE

What to do

- Discuss what people on the island say about the Birdman. (He is dangerous and mad; he puts spells on people; he is a spy.) Ask: *Why do you think people say those things? How is the Birdman isolated or different?* (He lives alone, wears strange clothes and talks to himself.)

- Hand out copies of photocopiable page 30 'Truth or rumour' to pairs. Ask them to counter each rumour with the truth, citing evidence from the novel.

- Arrange the children into two groups that form a long line, facing each other. One child plays the role of the Birdman and walks slowly between the lines as the children shout out rumours or accusations against him. Afterwards, ask the 'Birdman' to describe how the crowd made him/her feel.

- Repeat the exercise, but this time one line should shout out the accusations, and the other should counter each one and defend the Birdman. For example, if one child shouts out 'he signals to German submarines', one in the opposite line could counter with 'he is just trying to prevent shipwrecks'.

- Discuss how rumours can escalate, unless they are countered by the truth.

Support: Provide chapter/page references to help children find truths about the Birdman.
Extension: Broaden the discussion on rumour with reference to social media: how it can affect others' and their own well-being and discussing ways to manage it.

4. Daniel Pender

To ask questions to improve understanding.
To draw inferences, such as inferring characters' feelings, thoughts and motives from their actions.

Printable page 'Daniel Pender', copies of *Why the Whales Came*.

PSHE

What to do

- Ask: *How and why is Daniel Pender important to the plot of the novel? How is his character different from Gracie's?* Brainstorm some words and phrases to describe Daniel (brave, bold, fearless, independent, down to earth, and so on).

- Hand out copies of the printable page 'Daniel Pender'. Ask the children to work in pairs to complete the activity.

- Next, write the following three headings on the board: Description, Dialogue and Action.

- Ask the pairs to find examples of descriptions of Daniel in the book. List the best suggestions under the first heading on the board. Repeat the exercise for examples of dialogue and actions that reveal his character. Again, list the best suggestions on the board.

- Discuss as a class (referring to the board and the printable page) how the author builds the character using different devices, such as description, dialogue and action.

Support: Model examples of description, dialogue and actions before pairs begin scanning the novel.
Extension: Pairs could compare Daniel and Gracie in more detail, or compare Daniel to a character in another book they have read.

5. Beside the sea

Objectives

To draw inferences and justify them with evidence. To identify themes.

What you need

Copies of *Why the Whales Came*, media resource 'Navy recruitment poster'.

Cross-curricular link

Geography, science

What to do

- With the class, read the passage in Chapter 6 from 'It was while we were working side by side in the boatshed…' to 'I've taken the King's Shilling'. Elicit what provokes Mr Jenkins to enlist, and display the media resource 'Navy recruitment poster'. Ask the children to pick out all the references throughout the novel, direct or implied, to boats or the sea (for example, Gracie and Daniel working in the boatshed, the navy ships, Gracie and her mother fishing).

- The author once said of the Scilly islanders that 'the sea rules their lives'. What did he mean by this? Explain that sea conditions/tide times still rule the islanders' lives. Explain the terms 'high-water mark', 'high tide' and 'low tide'. Ask: *Why should these be so important to islanders?* (They use the sea for fishing and transport, and the tides can determine where and when boats can land.)

- Discuss which events in the plot are driven by the sea (Gracie's father joining the navy, the timber, the whales, the shipwreck). Ask: *Are there any plot elements that are not dependent on the sea?* (Examples include the friendship between the children and the Birdman.)

Differentiation

Support: Provide definitions for tricky vocabulary ('salvo', 'freighter') and technical/scientific terms.
Extension: Children could work in pairs to skim and scan the novel for more references to the sea and how it affects the islanders' lives.

6. Why whales?

Objectives

To use spoken language to develop understanding through imagining and exploring ideas. To identify themes and conventions.

What you need

Copies of *Why the Whales Came*.

What to do

- Read together the final part of Chapter 10, beginning 'I was sitting breathless in the sand' to the end. Ask: *What does the Birdman mean when he says, 'Oh please God, not again.' What is he trying to prevent?* (another massacre of whales)

- The following activities are discussion based. Allow children to discuss the question in pairs or small groups before discussing their ideas as a class.

- Refer to the book's title and ask the children if they can answer the question it poses. Ask: *How does the coming of the whales redeem the islanders from the curse on Samson?* With the class, consider how this gives the plot a 'cyclical' structure, centred on the coming of the whales.

- Discuss different views about whales expressed in the story. (Big Tim sees them as meat and ivory; the Birdman wants to protect them.) Which view do the children think the author takes, and why? Encourage them to support their arguments with evidence. For example, once the whales have been saved, Gracie's father returns home and people can visit Samson without fear.

- Ask questions such as: *What do you think the author's message is with reference to this particular event?* (If we do right by nature, nature will do right by us.)

Differentiation

Support: Emphasise the pattern in the plot by listing key events and repercussions on the board.
Extension: Encourage children to explore similar themes and conventions in other novels by the author, for example, the orangutan hunt in *Kensuke's Kingdom*.

7. Storyboard

Objective

To identify main ideas drawn from more than one paragraph and summarise these.

What you need

Copies of *Why the Whales Came*.

Cross-curricular link

Art & design

What to do

- Read Chapter 11 from 'Suddenly Mother was beside me…' to the end of the chapter. Ask the children to discuss the events described in this extract, summarising how the whales are saved and what happens to the Birdman.

- Tell the children that they are going to imagine that they are planning this extract for a film. Explain that filmmakers often make storyboards before filming – a sequence of pictures showing how the action develops.

- Arrange the children in pairs and let them re-read the passage. Encourage them to decide which scenes they are going to illustrate for their storyboard. Tell them to list six scenes and to write brief notes on what each scene should portray.

- Once they have done this, bring the class back together and write some of their suggestions on the board. Discuss some detail from each scene, for example, the Birdman and others wading into the sea in the dark toward the whales, waving torches.

- Let the children, in their pairs, draw the storyboards they have briefed.

Differentiation

Support: Model the first scene or two on the board before they begin.
Extension: Pairs could choose and storyboard another episode from the novel, or they could write a script to go with their storyboard.

8. Happy endings

Objective

To identify themes and conventions.

What you need

Copies of *Why the Whales Came*, photocopiable page 31 'Scilly tales'.

What to do

- Discuss superstition implicit in the main plot: that the islanders on Samson did a wrong by slaughtering the whales, and were punished with hunger and shipwreck. Encourage children to consider superstitions in the context of the time and setting: the novel is set in the early 1900s and the islanders live in a small, remote community where superstition might flourish.

- Challenge the children to explain how the ending of the story reinforces superstitious belief. (As the Birdman foretells, once the wrong is put right, everything comes good again.)

- Suggest that the happy ending is reminiscent of a folk or fairy tale. Can the children identify any other folk or fairytale features? (For example, the cyclical tale of the whales returning; the misunderstood 'monster' – the Birdman – who is really kind and gentle.)

- Hand out the photocopiable page 31 'Scilly tales' and ask the children to work in pairs to complete it.

- Bring the class back together to discuss ways that the novel differs from a fairy tale (for example, real-life setting, historical context, believable characters, first-person narrator). Ask: *Which other genre might it fit into?* (an adventure story)

Differentiation

Support: Work through the photocopiable sheet as a class before pairs begin to complete it themselves, checking that children understand the key aspects of plot.
Extension: Let pairs identify which aspects make the novel an adventure story, using the photocopiable sheet to frame their ideas.

Turning points

- Explain how each of the following drives events in the plot.
- Then cut out and glue the boxes in the order in which they feature in the story.

✂

A stranded whale
Windy weather at Popplestone Bay
A bad storm
A famine
Sudden fog
A submarine attack

Truth or rumour?

- Each statement below is a rumour about the Birdman that appears in the story.
- Oppose each rumour with a true fact about the Birdman and support each fact with evidence.

1. He eats cats and dogs.

_____

_____

2. He puts spells on people.

_____

_____

3. He is mad (he talks to himself).

_____

_____

4. He signals to German submarines.

_____

_____

5. He only comes out at night.

_____

_____

Scilly tales

● Explain how the following fairytale elements feature in the novel.

1. A 'kind' monster

_____

_____

2. A wrong punished

_____

_____

3. A kindness rewarded

_____

_____

4. A circular or cyclical tale

_____

_____

5. A happy ending

_____

_____

TALK ABOUT IT

1. A Isles of Scilly childhood

Objectives

To articulate and justify answers, arguments and opinions. To use spoken language to develop understanding through speculating and exploring ideas.

What you need

Copies of *Why the Whales Came*, photocopiable page 35 'Childhood'.

Cross-curricular link

History

What to do

- Read together the first part of Chapter 3, up to 'another message for us in the sand'.

- Discuss what we learn about Gracie and Daniel's lives on Bryher. Ask: *Why do they sometimes miss school?* (to help with fishing and other work) *Which chores do they help with?* (sweeping out the boatsheds, fishing for lobster bait, mending lobster pots)

- Read Chapter 6 together, from 'It was from Mr Wellbeloved' to 'the Birdman's cottage on Heathy Hill'. Ask: *What do we learn about the children's schooling?* (The teacher uses a blackboard; lessons are in arithmetic or about the war.) Ask how teachers and parents discipline children in the novel. (Mr Wellbeloved gives Gracie tables to write out; Daniel's father threatens him with 'the strap'.) Remind the children that the novel is set in 1914 when corporal punishment was widely practised.

- Ask the children to work individually to complete photocopiable page 35 'Childhood'. When they have finished, discuss their findings as a class. How are their lives different from Daniel's and Gracie's?

Differentiation

Support: Write the key facts about Gracie and Daniel's childhood for children to refer to.
Extension: Children can debate in small groups which things they prefer about their own lives, and which they prefer about Gracie's and Daniel's lives.

2. Sign language

Objectives

To use spoken language to develop understanding through speculating, hypothesising, imagining and exploring ideas. To draw inferences, such as inferring characters' feeling, thoughts and motives.

What you need

Copies of *Why the Whales Came*, media resource 'British Sign Language'.

What to do

- Read Chapter 4 from 'It was one long room' to the end. Ask the children why the Birdman's speech sounds strange (he is deaf) and how he lost his hearing (from a fever as a child).

- Ask: *What sounds do you think the Birdman would miss on the island?* List ideas on the board: waves, seagulls, fire crackling, hens, Prince barking.

- Ask: *How do the children first communicate with him?* (They write in the sand/on paper; speak so he can lip-read.)

- Do the children know about finger spelling or sign language? Display the finger-spelling guide from the media resource 'British Sign Language' and encourage the children to spell their own name.

- Read Chapter 6 from 'I myself was never comfortable…' to 'less and less as the months passed'. Ask: *Can you describe the picture language that Daniel and the Birdman invent? How similar or different is it from British sign language?* (Look at the second screen of the media resource.)

- Write some words on the board, such as 'waves', 'seagull', 'fishing', 'woodcarving'. Let small groups design picture signs for these words. Invite volunteers to show their signs.

Differentiation

Support: Model an example, using picture language to represent a bird or waves.
Extension: Challenge groups to choose more words or ideas from the novel and devise signs for them. Then let other groups guess their meaning.

3. Right and wrong

Objective

To participate in role play and improvisations.

What you need

Copies of *Why the Whales Came*, photocopiable page 36 'White lies'.

Cross-curricular link

PSHE

What to do

- Read Chapter 5. Ask the children to explain why the islanders are committing a felony. (The timber is the Crown's property and they 'steal' it.) Ask: *How does Gracie justify this?* (The islanders are poor and survive by salvaging materials like this.)

- Invite small groups to improvise a short scene about a group of islanders (including Gracie's father) finding the timber and deciding what to do with it. One member of the group might have reservations and another might be afraid of getting caught by the Preventative. Allow the groups time to plan and practise, then invite one or two to perform to the class. Freeze-frame the drama at points of conflict and ask the class to decide how others might persuade them to go ahead and hide the timber. Afterwards, discuss whether they think the islanders were right or wrong to take the timber.

- Suggest that Gracie and Daniel fib or disobey rules/ instructions several times in the story. Hand out copies of photocopiable page 36 'White lies' and ask the children to work in pairs to complete it.

- Discuss the children's findings as a class. Discuss whether they think that telling white lies might sometimes be justified, for example, to help dispel unjustified prejudices against the Birdman.

Differentiation

Support: Consider the first two questions on the sheet together before pairs begin work.
Extension: Use the sheet to prompt a discussion on how far the plot would change if the children did not fib or disobey any orders.

4. The Great War

Objectives

To use spoken language to develop understanding through exploring ideas.
To participate in discussions.

What you need

Copies of *Why the Whales Came*, media resource 'WWI images'.

Cross-curricular link

History

What to do

- Read Chapter 6 as far as 'at the end of the day'. Ask the children what they know about World War I. Briefly outline the main facts: the dates (1914–1918); what triggered it (the assassination of the Austrian Archduke Franz Ferdinand); where it was fought (largely in continental Europe); and the countries involved (UK and her allies versus Germany and her allies). Explain that the war was fought on land, sea and – for the first time – in the air.

- Refer to the text and discuss the 'fronts' along which the armies fought in Europe, mentioning the trenches. Display the photographs from media resource 'WWI images' to highlight trenches, weapons and the home front.

- Explain that Tresco was a base for seaplanes hunting for German submarines. Can they suggest why? (The seaplanes could warn of submarines before they reached the south coast of England.)

- In pairs or small groups, discuss how the war changes people's lives in the novel before sharing ideas (the call-up, blackout, fear of submarines, food shortages). Ask: *How does wartime change people's feelings and behaviour?* (There are increased feelings of patriotism, prejudices and fear.)

Differentiation

Support: Write keywords and phrases on the board to prompt discussion (food shortages, King's Shilling, submarines).
Extension: Let children investigate more about other aspects of life on Scilly during World War I.

TALK ABOUT IT

5. Jobs on Bryher

Objective

To use spoken language to develop understanding through speculating and exploring ideas.

What you need

Copies of *Why the Whales Came*, media resource 'Working life on the Isles of Scilly', photocopiable page 37 'Jobs on Bryher'.

Cross-curricular links

Geography, history

What to do

- Read through Chapter 7 as far as 'to bring in enough money to keep us going'.

- Discuss what we learn about the work people do on the island (farming, fishing for lobsters, gathering seaweed, keeping bees/harvesting honey). List some of the jobs, and the skills the islanders possess, on the board; refer to the images in the media resource 'Working life on the Isles of Scilly'.

- Discuss the resources available to the islanders (animals, fish, timber, seaweed, driftwood, and so on). Ask: *Which resources do they have to buy and what can they produce or find themselves?*

- Ask the children to identify jobs that are mainly done by men (boat building), by women (growing flowers) or by children (mending lobster pots).

- Provide copies of photocopiable page 37 'Jobs on Bryher' and ask the children to work in pairs to complete it. When they have finished, bring the class back together and encourage speculation on the different jobs people do on the Isles of Scilly today, and how much they may have changed or stayed the same since Gracie's day.

Differentiation

Support: List key jobs and materials on the board as children discuss them.

Extension: Let pairs use the internet to explore jobs on the Isles of Scilly today and design another table on the other side of the photocopiable sheet listing them under headings.

6. The bully

Objectives

To participate in discussions and role play.
To consider and evaluate different viewpoints.

What you need

Copies of *Why the Whales Came*.

Cross-curricular link

PSHE

What to do

- Read Chapter 9 from 'In assembly…' to 'And he was gone'. Discuss different aspects of Tim's bullying (pushing, hurting, name-calling, picking on someone smaller/younger than himself). Ask the children if they can cite any other episodes from the story that show Tim to be a bully. (Tim and his gang attack Gracie and Daniel's boats; they ransack the Birdman's cottage.)

- Now read Chapter 10 from 'I was woken suddenly' to 'we've got to warn him quick'. Recap on why Tim and his gang might pick on the Birdman (he lives alone, he is deaf, he dresses strangely, and there are rumours and tales about him). Remind the children that wartime can increase prejudices and tensions.

- Arrange the children into small groups and tell them to prepare a short drama about Big Tim and his gang planning the dawn attack – but include Daniel, who has overheard them and is arguing against it.

- Invite one or two of the groups to perform their scene, and then discuss the issues it raises. Ask: *How did it feel to be Daniel? Why is it easier to bully in a gang?*

Differentiation

Support: Note on the board keywords and phrases from the extracts to help children voice Big Tim's views.

Extension: Let children skim and scan the novel for all relevant text to help them voice Big Tim's views and opinions.

Childhood

- Make notes about your life in the mind map below.
- Use it to compare and contrast your life with Gracie's and Daniel's lives.

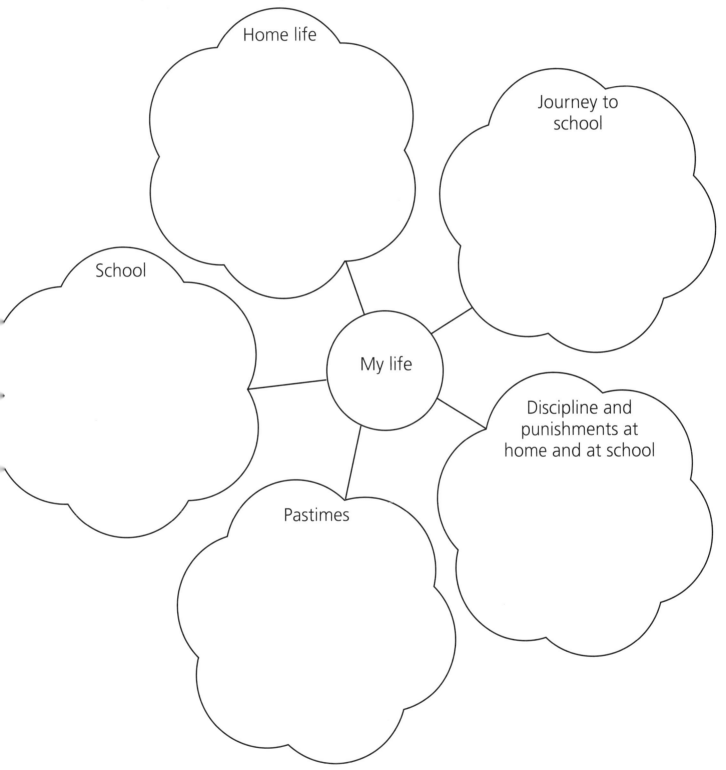

- On the reverse of this sheet of paper, draw a mind map for Gracie's and Daniel's lives. Make notes about their lives, comparing and contrasting their lives with yours.

White lies

- In the boxes, explain why Gracie and Daniel break each rule.
- State why you think they were right or wrong in the speech bubbles.

They visit the 'forbidden' side of the island because	I think they were right/wrong because
They make contact with the Birdman because	I think they were right/wrong because
They lie about who made the cormorant because	I think they were right/wrong because
They play truant because	I think they were right/wrong because

- Think of two more rules that were broken by Daniel and Gracie. Write about these on the other side of this sheet of paper and explain why you think they were right or wrong to break them.

- Think about any rules at home or school that you have broken and explain why you think it was right or fair to break them.

Jobs on Bryher

● Make notes in the table below about the different jobs and activities done on Bryher.

Job	Who does it	Skills needed	Resources needed/produced
Farming			
Fishing			
Boat building			
Beachcombing			

GET WRITING

1. Holiday island

To discuss writing similar to that which they are planning to write in order to understand and learn from its structure, vocabulary and grammar. To use simple organisational devices in non-narrative material.

What you need

Copies of *Why the Whales Came*, brochures on the Isle of Scilly, photocopiable page 41 'Tourist information'.

What to do

- Read together Chapter 1 from 'The beach on the sheltered coast…' to 'none of us ever did'. Refer to the map at the start of the book to identify named places – Rushy Bay, Shipman's Head, and so on.

- Tell the children they are going to plan a tourist brochure or website about Bryher. Display brochures about the Isles of Scilly (and other tourism websites) and discuss the emotive language typical of the genre – picturesque cottages, turquoise seas. Discuss how you might edit Gracie's description for tourists (for example, taking out references to the dangerous west coast and emphasising the calmer seas on the east coast, or describing the black cliffs as 'dramatic rocky scenery').

- In pairs, ask the children to scan the text for ideas for their brochure or website. Then bring the class together and list their suggestions on the board.

- Hand out copies of photocopiable page 41 'Tourist information' for the children to complete. Invite them to draw on the novel for more ideas.

- Once they have completed the photocopiable sheet, invite some children to share their ideas.

- A follow-up lesson or homework time will be needed for children to use their plans to create a final poster, brochure or website.

Differentiation

Support: Skim and scan the text together as a class, listing key facts on the board; children could create a poster rather than a brochure.

2. A day in the life

Objective

To learn the conventions of writing a diary.

What you need

Copies of *Why the Whales Came*, photocopiable page 42 'Zachariah's diary'.

What to do

- Read together Chapter 4. Tell the children that they are going to write a diary entry that the Birdman might write about the day. Ask them to summarise the main events: spending the night on Samson with Prince; rowing back in a gale; finding the timber; returning to the cottage to find Gracie and Daniel; and learning from them about the outbreak of war.

- Encourage the children to think about how the Birdman might feel (tired after rowing against the wind, pleased that the children have come, upset to hear about the outbreak of war).

- Ask the children to suggest other things that the Birdman would do in the day (such as baking bread, feeding the hens and goats, woodcarving).

- Hand out copies of photocopiable page 42 'Zachariah's diary'. Ask the children to complete it, referring back to the text for detail. Discuss how a personal diary is usually written in the first person.

- When they have finished this activity, invite volunteers to read out their work. Discuss how the same events (as recorded in Gracie's narrative) are seen from a different point of view.

Differentiation

Support: List the main events in the day on the board for children to refer to.
Extension: Children could try writing and comparing Gracie's or Daniel's diary for the same day.

3. Fog-bound

Objectives

To discuss writing similar to that which they are planning to write in order to understand and learn from its structure, vocabulary and grammar. To create an atmospheric setting.

What you need

Copies of *Why the Whales Came.*

Cross-curricular link

Geography

What to do

• Read Chapter 7 from 'We sat over our oars and drifted…' to 'all the more lasting'. Ask the children to explain Gracie and Daniel's predicament. (They are in a boat and lost at sea in thick fog.)

• Scanning the text together for descriptive words and phrases for sound, such as 'the wash of the sea' and 'the piping of invisible oystercatchers'. Ask: *Can you find any metaphors?* ('crack in the blackness', 'charge of the waves')

• Ask: *Which phrases are onomatopoeic?* ('the hiss of surf on the shingle', 'the whisper of waves') Ask: *Why does the author concentrate on the sense of hearing?* (The children can't see anything.)

• Re-read the sentence beginning 'The fog…' to examine personification. Ask the children to find words describing the fog ('obscure', 'shroud', 'impenetrable'). Can they explain what these words mean and suggest replacements?

• Tell the children they are going to imagine they are lost in fog. Ask them to write a short description in the first person, using a range of senses. Encourage them to use some of the techniques the author uses: onomatopoeia, alliteration and metaphor.

• Share some of the most effective paragraphs.

Differentiation

Support: Let children work in pairs to write some similes or metaphors to describe thick fog.
Extension: Challenge children to draft a short poem about thick fog in a place familiar to them.

4. A spy drama

Objective

To prepare playscripts to read aloud and to perform.

What you need

Copies of *Why the Whales Came.*

What to do

• Read Chapter 10 from 'It's Big Tim and his crowd' to 'for making him look a fool'. Tell the children that they are going to prepare a short drama in two scenes: the first, when Big Tim tells his father his suspicions; the second, when the police arrive at Daniel's house.

• As a shared activity, ask the children to identify the characters involved in each scene. Make a list of these names on the board.

• Ask the children to work in small groups to discuss what each character might say in the scene. Encourage them to consider how they are feeling (for example, Big Tim's angry suspicions, Daniel's frustration, his father's anger and the policemen's impatience.)

• Model a few lines of dialogue or refer to a playscript for the presentation of dialogue. Note that speech marks are not necessary.

• Give the children sufficient time to draft and practise their scenes, and then invite groups to perform their scenes for the rest of the class. Encourage constructive feedback on dialogue and presentation.

Differentiation

Support: Model a short dialogue on the board before children begin.

> **Tim:** He's a spy, Dad!
> **Father:** A spy? What makes you think that?
> **Tim:** He's been lighting fires. He's signalling to enemy submarines!

Extension: Encourage children to add detail to their script, including setting, stage directions, and so on.

GET WRITING

5. Narwhals

To retrieve, record and present information from non-fiction. To organise paragraphs around a theme.

What you need

Copies of *Why the Whales Came*, media resource 'Narwhal', internet or reference books.

What to do

- Read together Chapter 10 from 'The donkey and cart…' to 'It's the same, isn't it, Mr Woodcock?' Ask: *Can you recall the type of whale that is stranded?* (a narwhal) Display the photograph from the media resource 'Narwhal'.

- Ask small groups to re-read the passage, noting down key facts about narwhals (size, colour, markings, and so on). Tell them that they will be using these facts to write a report about narwhals. They should write anything else they remember about these whales from the novel.

- Bring the class together and list the facts on the board. Encourage the children to give other facts about whales (such as how they breathe or feed). Discuss how to organise the facts into paragraphs under appropriate headings, such as size, appearance or behaviour. Ask: *What other topics could be covered in a report?* (habitat, migration, diet, and so on) List headings on the board.

- Provide groups with access to the internet or reference books and ask them to find facts about narwhals. A note-taker in each group should organise the facts into paragraphs under headings.

- Share the children's findings. Write paragraph headings on the board, and discuss how the report would be structured: a general opening, a concluding statement and facts grouped by topic.

Differentiation

Support: Let children write bulleted facts about narwhals under appropriate headings.
Extension: Challenge children to draft a report on narwhals for a scientific book or website.

6. Famine on Samson

Objectives

To discuss and plan ideas. To use simple organisational devices in non-narrative material.

What you need

Interactive activity 'Samson's curse', copies of *Why the Whales Came*, photocopiable page 43 'Newspaper article'.

What to do

- Begin by challenging the children to complete the interactive activity 'Samson's curse'.

- Read Chapter 10 from 'Samson was always a poor place…' to 'your poor father's dead'. Ask the children to summarise what happened on Samson and what the Birdman implies (the island was cursed because of the massacre of the whales). Remind them that Gracie's father spoke about the troubles on Samson. Read together his account in Chapter 2, starting at 'The people of Samson woke up…' to 'his mother were alone on Samson'.

- Ask the children to list all the bad things that happened after the massacre of the whales. List suggestions on the board (shipwrecks, hunger, fever, the well drying up, and so on).

- Tell the children they are going to plan a newspaper report about the last people (the Birdman and his mother) leaving Samson. It should recount recent events and explain why people have left.

- Hand out copies of photocopiable page 43 'Newspaper article' for the children to complete.

- Bring the class back together to review their work. Discuss appropriate style and organisation for a news report (attention-grabbing headline, factual content, quotations from local people and son).

Differentiation

Support: Provide examples of newspaper reports about natural disasters affecting people's lives to help children understand the way in which a newspaper article is organised and written.
Extension: Challenge the children create a final version of their report, using computing skills.

Tourist information

- Use this sheet to plan a website aimed at tourists visiting Bryher.

http://www.holidayinBryher.co.uk

Menu

Visiting Bryher

Home

Bryher's history

Landscape and scenery

Weather

People

Things to do

Eating

Zachariah's diary

Write an entry for the Birdman's diary. Use the headings on the left to help you plan your writing.

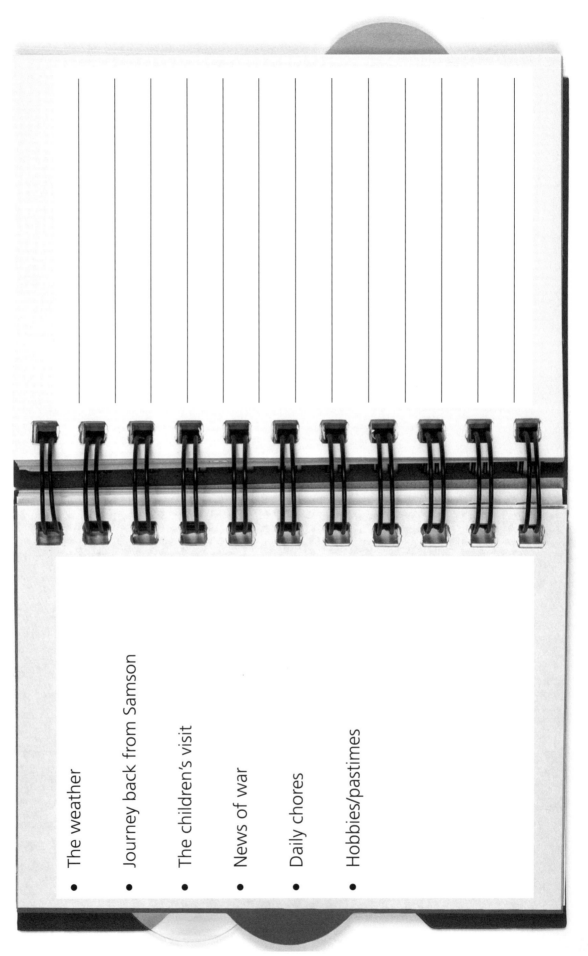

- The weather

- Journey back from Samson

- The children's visit

- News of war

- Daily chores

- Hobbies/pastimes

Newspaper article

● Use this sheet to write a newspaper article about people leaving the island.

The Scillies Herald

Headline

_____

_____

_____

_____

Brief the artwork or photo

A quote by Birdman's mother.

_____

_____

_____

_____

_____

_____

A quote by another islander affected by the fever or shipwreck.

_____

_____

▼ ASSESSMENT

1. What are they like?

Objectives

To draw inferences such as inferring characters' thoughts, feelings and motives from their actions, and justifying these with evidence. To participate in discussions and develop understanding through imagining and exploring ideas.

What you need

Flashcards with the names 'Gracie', 'Daniel', 'the Birdman' and 'Big Tim', copies of *Why the Whales Came.*

Cross-curricular link

PSHE

What to do

- Write 'the Birdman' on the board and challenge the children to think of three adjectives that best describe his character. Emphasise that they need to be able to back up their suggestions with evidence from the novel.

- List the best suggestions on the board. Encourage children to evaluate each suggestion. Ask, for example: *Is he lonely or is he happy without human company because Prince and the other animals keep him company? Is there any evidence in the novel that would support one or the other viewpoint?*

- Arrange the class into small groups. Display the flashcards, one at a time, allowing the children time to consider and list three adjectives that best describe each character. They must be able to back them up with evidence. A note-taker should take down their ideas.

- Bring the class back together and ask the note-taker from each group to suggest their words, writing the best suggestions on the board and reviewing different choices of word.

Differentiation

Support: Together compile a list of actions or events on the board for each character, to prompt descriptive words.
Extension: Add other topics to the flashcards, such as 'Samson' or 'narwhals'.

2. Wise words

Objective

To use spoken language to develop understanding through exploring ideas.

What you need

Copies of *Why the Whales Came*, printable page 'Wise words'.

What to do

- Tell the children they are going to focus on the friendship between the children and the Birdman. Write two headings on the board:
  - What does the Birdman learn from Gracie and Daniel?
  - What do Gracie and Daniel learn from the Birdman?

- In pairs, ask the children to scan the novel for ideas for each heading. List some of their ideas on the board. (For example, the Birdman learns about their families and the war; the children learn to question other people's prejudices.)

- Reflect on the wisdom of the Birdman's words, in view of the story ending.

- Discuss what brings wisdom: an open mind, being willing to learn, experience, age? Encourage children to refer to their own and others' experience, to cite examples of what they perceive as wisdom.

- Hand out copies of the printable page. Challenge children, in pairs, to identify the speakers and discuss if they are wise words or not in the context of the story. Ask them to say whether they agree with the words, backing up their answers with reasons.

Differentiation

Support: Work through the printable page as a class activity, providing a list of names for children to match with the speakers:
1 – Mrs Jenkins; 2 and 3 – the Birdman;
4 – Mr Jenkins; 5 – Gracie; 6 – Daniel.
Extension: Ask pairs to draft some of their own wise words to advise or guide younger children.

3. Radio play

Objectives

To prepare playscripts. To create settings.

What you need

Copies of *Why the Whales Came*.

What to do

- Challenge the children to create a playscript for a radio adaptation of the novel, focusing on the scene when Gracie and Daniel explore the ruined cottages on Samson. Remind them that they will need to evoke the scene by voices and sounds only, so that listeners can imagine the setting.

- Tell them to re-read Chapter 8 from 'It seemed that on Samson it was the terns that decided' to 'and ran out after him'. They need to focus on action, dialogue and setting.

- Allow them time to plan the action: the children whistling for Prince, then coming across the cottages, exploring them and discovering the narwhal horn. Encourage them to keep dialogue concise but also to convey emotions, for example, Gracie's fears or the children's fascination with the horn.

- They should also list sound effects that will help to evoke the scene: the noisy terns, the sound of the children whistling for Prince, the sound of the waves or of limpet shells crunching underfoot.

- When they are ready, they should draft a playscript, inserting stage directions and sound effects appropriately.

Differentiation

Support: Use notes on the board as a planning aid before they begin drafting.
Extension: Children could choose another scene to adapt as a playscript for radio.

4. What's the big idea?

Objective

To identify themes and conventions.

What you need

Photocopiable page 47 'Top themes'.

What to do

- Begin by asking the children to identify the main themes of the novel.

- Ask them to support their suggestions with reasons, for example, 'I think looking after animals and the natural world is the main theme because saving the whales means there is a happy ending'; 'I think giving everyone a chance is the main theme because the children find out that the Birdman is really a kind person'.

- Write their suggestions for themes on the board and discuss which, if any, they would identify as the most important theme, again encouraging them to give reasons.

- Provide each child with a copy of the photocopiable page 47 'Top themes' and tell the children to fill it in, working in pairs or individually. Encourage them to use the other side of the page to write any other themes or ideas that the novel contains that have not been covered, if possible using the same pattern of asserting a belief.

- Bring the class back together to review their findings.

Differentiation

Support: Work through the photocopiable sheet as a shared activity, making brief notes on the board before the children begin writing.
Extension: Invite children to work in pairs to compare and contrast the main themes with those in other novels by the author they are familiar with.

5. Perfect punctuation

Objective

To use and punctuate direct speech.

What you need

Printable page 'Wanted – punctuation', copies of *Why the Whales Came*.

What to do

- Remind the children of their work in lesson 5 of the 'Grammar, punctuation and spelling' section ('Just imagine') on writing and punctuating direct speech. Tell them that they are going to try punctuating extracts taken from the novel.

- Hand out copies of the printable page 'Wanted – punctuation'. Arrange the children into pairs and tell them to read the sentences carefully and then attempt to write them out using capital letters and correct punctuation.

- Allow them time to complete the task. Then bring the class back together to review their work and check their punctuation against that in the novel (1 = Chapter 2; 2 = Chapter 4; 3 = Chapter 5; 4 = Chapter 8; 5 = Chapter 10; 6 = Chapter 11).

- Encourage them to reflect on the trickiest aspects of the task, and any punctuation marks they missed or are incorrect.

- Can they suggest what the correct punctuation marks add, apart from helping us to read the sentences more easily? (Punctuation can, for example, frame a question or indicate a tone of voice, as with Big Tim's expression of astonishment.)

Differentiation

Support: Read the sentences through as a class before pairs begin, briefly revising the use of capitals for new sentences and proper names, and possessive apostrophes.

Extension: Challenge pairs to work together, each choosing more sentences from the novel to dictate, for their partner to write down and punctuate.

6. The whales quiz

Objectives

To articulate and justify answers, arguments and opinions. To participate in discussions and presentations.

What you need

Interactive activity 'Whales quiz', copies of *Why the Whales Came*.

What to do

- Tell the children they are going to try answering a multiple-choice quiz about the novel. Let them attempt the quiz using the interactive activity 'Whales quiz', working in small groups: they should discuss their answers and come to a consensus before selecting the answer.

- When they have finished, challenge groups to compile their own quiz questions using the novel. They could attempt another multiple-choice quiz, or write statements for a 'true or false' quiz.

- Model some examples on the board:
  - The Birdman's donkey is called Prince. [False]
  - Gracie hides the cormorant in the roof. [True]

- Groups can then challenge each other to answer their quiz questions. When they have finished, review scores and announce winning teams or groups. (Each group will have to write the same number of questions.)

- Encourage feedback, identifying which quiz questions were most challenging and why.

Differentiation

Support: Model further questions for each type of quiz on the board before groups begin, and brainstorm some quiz questions or statements together.

Extension: Groups can attempt to devise more difficult or challenging quizzes about the novel; they could create a quiz show or a class quiz with various 'rounds' on different topics.

Top themes

● Explain how each of the following beliefs features as a theme in the novel.

1. Look after the natural world and it will look after you.

_____

_____

2. Don't always believe what others tell you.

_____

_____

3. White lies can sometimes be justified.

_____

_____

4. Friendship can overcome prejudice.

_____

_____

5. It is right to stand up to bullies.

_____

_____

6. Kindness will be rewarded; cruelty will be punished.

_____

_____

SCHOLASTIC

Available in this series:

978-1407-16066-5

978-1407-16053-5

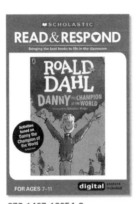

978-1407-16054-2

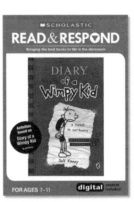

978-1407-16055-9

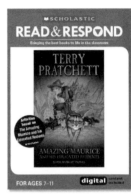

978-1407-16056-6

978-1407-16057-3

978-1407-16058-0

978-1407-16059-7

978-1407-16060-3

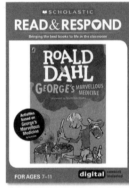

978-1407-16061-0

978-1407-16062-7

978-1407-16063-4

978-1407-16064-1

978-1407-16065-8

978-1407-16052-8

978-1407-16067-2

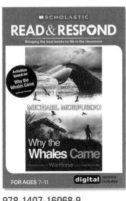

978-1407-16068-9

978-1407-16069-6

978-1407-16070-2

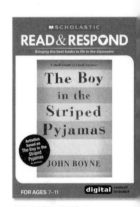

978-1407-16071-9

To find out more, call: 0845 6039091
or visit our website www.scholastic.co.uk/readandrespond